4

E-BOY

ANH DO

A NEW GEMINI

E-BOY

4

Illustrations by Tim McEwen

ALLEN&UNWIN

SYDNEY • MELBOURNE • AUCKLAND • LONDON

First published by Allen & Unwin in 2022

Allen & Unwin
83 Alexander Street
Crows Nest NSW 2065
Cammaraygal
Australia
Phone: (61 2) 8425 0100
Email: info@allenandunwin.com
Web: www.allenandunwin.com

*Allen & Unwin acknowledges the Traditional Owners of the lands
on which we live and work. We pay our respects to all Aboriginal and
Torres Strait Islander Elders, past and present.*

A catalogue record for this
book is available from the
National Library of Australia

NATIONAL
LIBRARY
OF AUSTRALIA

ISBN 978 1 76087 903 7

For teaching resources, explore www.allenandunwin.com/resources/
for-teachers

Cover design by Jo Hunt
Cover illustrations by Tim McEwen
Additional illustrative work by Chris Wahl
Text design by Jo Hunt
Set in 13/22 pt Legacy Serif Std by Jo Hunt

Printed and bound in Australia by McPherson's Printing Group

10 9 8 7 6 5 4 3 2 1

The paper in this book is FSC® certified.
FSC® promotes environmentally responsible,
socially beneficial and economically viable
management of the world's forests.

MIX
Paper from
responsible sources
FSC® C001695

CHAPTER 1

Ethan and Gemini stared at each other.

Gemini let go of the plane with one hand, and Penny saw his fingertips begin to glow. *He's going to use his laser scalpels!*

Ethan remained frozen with fear. Gemini strained against the wind of the flight to bring his hand to the glass, beams blazing from his fingers.

Penny screamed, 'ETHAN!' and grabbed the control wheel, hauling it sideways.

The plane rolled, flipping upside down, back up, then upside down again. The lasers vanished, and Gemini grabbed back onto the plane as it spun through the sky.

'Ethan, I can't fly this thing!' shouted Penny.

Ethan struggled to sit up in his seat, then snatched at the control wheel to straighten the path of the plane.

Thumps came from outside the plane as Gemini regained his footing. When Ethan looked at the plane's readouts he didn't understand them, but when he closed his eyes he felt what they were saying about the plane's position, speed and altitude. He also felt where Gemini was.

'Hold on,' Ethan said, and sent the plane into another spiral.

For a few minutes, the plane spun and dipped, levelled out, then whirled and dipped again. Gemini would cling on as the plane jagged through the sky, then climb forwards again as soon as it flew straight.

Ethan spoke without opening his eyes. 'I can't keep this up. We'll run out of fuel.'

Penny saw that Ethan was covered in sweat, his nose bleeding. She mopped at his face with her sleeve as the plane evened out. As Gemini's hand came back into view on the windscreen, Penny gazed at it in fear . . . and then looked past it to a thick grey cloud.

'There's rain ahead,' she said. 'Maybe that'll help shake him off!'

Ethan searched through the plane's systems – a weather radar was in the nosecone. Tapping into it, he could sense the storm ahead. He aimed the plane straight at it, then sent it into a spin again.

Ethan slumped down in his seat as Penny gripped the sides of hers. Ethan tried to focus on the plane's systems as it pitched and rolled; Penny could only focus on not vomiting.

Ethan felt the plane using more fuel as it twisted through the air. Penny heard Gemini thumping against the fuselage as the twirling flung him this way and that. The plane entered the stormcloud and all was grey, rain coming from every direction.

Penny could barely tell if they'd been in the cloud for five seconds or five minutes when the plane burst back into sunlight. Ethan immediately turned the wheel sharply.

'Is he—' said Penny.

'He's still there,' said Ethan as the plane plunged back into the grey.

Penny tried closing her eyes, but that made the backflips of her stomach worse. The thumps continued. One blow hit louder, and Penny looked up to see a bulge in the ceiling about the size and shape of a foot.

Ethan sent the plane straight up and spinning. It rotated faster and faster, until Penny saw something falling towards the ground below and gasped, 'He's off!'

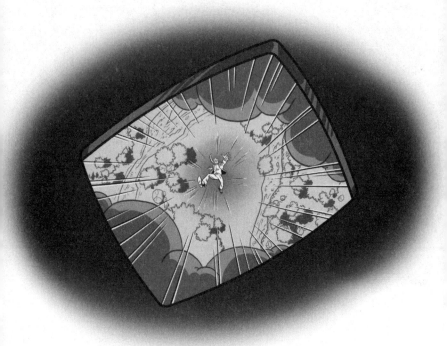

Ethan's head lolled. The plane stopped spinning, but kept climbing.

'Ethan, are you okay?' Penny asked.

Ethan gave an exhausted smile, then blacked out.

The plane's speed carried it upwards a little further, then gravity took over and it started to fall. Penny shut her eyes again, this time more terrified than nauseous as she realised the engines had all shut down along with Ethan.

She reached out to shake Ethan back into consciousness, but he was completely limp. The plane whined and shook through the air as it plummeted.

Penny thought about when she had first met Ethan, first arranged for Gemini to perform

surgery on him that was too difficult for even the most skilled of human hands. She'd never imagined it would lead to the adventures that it had, or to the two of them being about to crash a plane in Bombara . . .

Then she felt a lurch in their flightpath as the engines started up again.

Penny opened her eyes. The lights in the plane were on, the instruments and readouts were glowing, and Ethan was sitting in the pilot's seat upright and bright-eyed.

The plane steadied, soaring as gracefully as ever.

'Ethan?'

'Penny, I . . . I feel amazing!' said Ethan. 'I haven't felt this good in weeks!'

Penny smiled for a moment, but the smile faded quickly.

'Gemini,' she said haltingly. 'He must've hit the ground and ... deactivated. The link between him and you is broken.'

'You mean I'm cured?'

'Yes.'

'Fantastic! We don't have to run from him anymore, I'll be back to normal, we can relax a bit and—'

'We need to go back,' Penny interrupted. 'We need to find him.'

'What?'

Penny took a deep breath. 'Ethan, we can't just leave Gemini there. He is still linked to you somehow. His wellbeing is your wellbeing.'

'But he's probably broken anyhow – I mean, what are we going to do with him?' Ethan protested.

'The person we were coming here to see is the best person to fix him,' Penny replied.

'I thought she was gonna help me!' The plane shook a little, responding to Ethan's anger and confusion.

'She knows medicine and robotics, like me. She taught me both before she left for Bombara, where she could keep experimenting without as many restrictions as back home in Titus. She can help you both.'

Ethan shook his head. 'Gemini has been following us, trying to kill us, and now that we're finally free you want to go back to find him?'

Penny gestured at the fuel gauge. 'We need to land, Ethan. Soon.'

Ethan gritted his teeth. He was feeling strong again. He wanted to get back to helping his parents. But he knew deep down inside that Penny was right.

Ethan took them below the clouds and looked through the camera mounted on the undercarriage of the plane. They were flying over a field that was full of cows and surrounded by trees. There was no sign of Gemini at first, but then he saw that one tree had broken branches.

'Okay, I might know where he is,' said Ethan. 'Now for the ugly bit.'

Ethan had played the occasional flight simulator when he was younger, but that was nothing like this. He aimed the plane at the straightest patch of grassland he could find, then started to ease it down.

Ethan closed his eyes, and Penny had a familiar moment of panic before she remembered the instruments and cameras were way more useful to him through his powers than by looking at them.

As the plane approached the ground, Ethan lowered the wheels, kept the nose high and held his breath.

The plane thumped into the ground, bouncing Ethan and Penny around in their seats until it skidded to a stop.

Ethan and Penny sat for a moment, staring straight through the windscreen, then began to laugh in relief. Ethan unclipped his seatbelt, his left arm feeling strong. He was on his feet and opening the cockpit before Penny had released herself from her seat.

Once outside, Ethan led Penny in the direction of the damaged tree.

A short walk later, they were at the foot of the tree. It was dotted by stripped bark and broken branches, and lying in a heap at the bottom was Gemini. Penny gasped to see him, twisted awkwardly and unmoving.

Ethan and Penny lifted him up.

'He's so heavy!' said Ethan. Sweat dripped off both of them in the humidity.

They half-carried, half-dragged Gemini back to the plane. Even feeling his strongest, Ethan strained to haul Gemini's dead weight up the steps into the aircraft.

They heaved him into a seat. Penny strapped him in while Ethan returned to the pilot's position. Ethan looked out the window and frowned as Penny settled in the co-pilot's seat. 'What's wrong?' she asked.

'The landing gear got damaged when we landed,' Ethan said. 'I'm not sure how we're gonna get fast enough to take off.'

He started the plane and closed his eyes. He felt his way through the plane to the landing gear, and found the wires and hydraulics that moved the wheels. Ethan concentrated and the wires twisted and pulled, straightening the bent metal under the plane.

'This is impressive, even for you,' said Penny, feeling the plane shift beneath them.

'I know!' said Ethan. 'I've never felt stronger!'

Extra wiring wrapped itself around the damaged struts to strengthen them, and Ethan moved his mind to the plane's controls and set them in motion. The field wasn't as smooth as a runway – the vibrations shook Ethan and Penny to their bones as they picked up speed – but Ethan still managed to guide the plane back into the sky.

CHAPTER 2

As they flew on, Penny filled Ethan in on her old mentor. Professor Jackie Moore was renowned around the world for her brilliance in experimenting with combining robotics and people.

She'd left Titus when the government seemed to be forming divided opinions about

her work. Some thought it should be stopped; others thought her ideas would be better used by the army than in hospitals. Her facilities in Bombara weren't as state-of-the-art, but at least the government left her alone.

Penny didn't have Professor Moore's address, but she had coordinates for the location of the lab. She gave Ethan a list of numbers that meant nothing to him, but he used his power to feed them into the plane's navigation system and away they went.

In less than an hour, Ethan said, 'We're getting close.' He looked out the window, and then through the cameras to the tropical jungle below. 'I don't see anywhere to land, though.'

A moment later, he gave a fist-pump of relief. Cut into the jungle was a small landing strip, and near it were three small buildings almost covered by trees.

Ethan brought the plane around and aimed it at the tiny runway. Having landed the plane once, he felt better about setting it down a second time . . .

Until the damaged landing gear touched down and one wheel broke away completely.

Ethan fought the controls as the left wing crashed into the ground, dragging the plane towards one of the buildings. A grey-haired woman wearing a white coat ran out the door.

The wing carved a deep groove into the ground and then hit a building with a thud.

Just as the woman reached the plane, the door flew open and Ethan and Penny tumbled out at her feet.

'Are you both okay?' the woman asked, then looked closer. 'Penny, is that you?!'

Penny didn't answer, she just took the grey-haired woman's hand and pulled her into a big hug.

'Ethan,' Penny said over the other woman's shoulder, 'this is Professor Jackie Moore, one of the most amazing scientists on the planet.'

'Are you guys okay?' Professor Moore repeated.

'We're fine,' said Penny.

Penny noticed the professor looking at Ethan.

'This is Ethan, a friend of mine. He has amazing abilities.'

'Amazing ... abilities ... but why are you here? I mean, it's wonderful to see you, but ...'

'Come,' said Penny.

Ethan opened the door of the plane and Penny led Professor Moore in. Still strapped in the seat was Gemini.

'Who's this, is he . . .' Professor Moore said. 'He's . . . not human, is he?'

'No,' said Penny.

'Did you make him?' Professor Moore looked Gemini over. 'He's pretty badly damaged.'

'That's why we're here,' said Penny. 'I hope we didn't damage your lab when we landed.'

Professor Moore smiled. 'No, no, not at all. You may have dented my bedroom a little, though. Let's go talk.'

Over the next hour, Ethan did nothing but look on amazed. Penny gave the professor a USB stick with Gemini's schematics, and the two discussed how to carry out the needed repairs. Professor Moore filled notebook after notebook with details of Gemini's construction. They both spoke so fast that Ethan had trouble keeping up.

Ethan helped carry Gemini into the lab. It was tiny, with barely enough room to move around the big metal slab in the centre. Various electronic instruments hung from the ceiling.

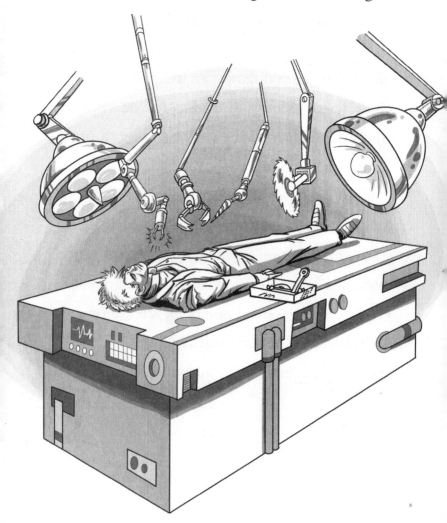

Penny took Ethan back outside. 'I'm sorry,' she said. 'The lab is only big enough for Jackie and me to work in. You'll need to wait out here. There's a TV in the dining area.'

'Awesome,' Ethan said sarcastically, frowning at the thought of being pushed aside for Gemini yet again.

'You'll have company – there's an assistant,' said Penny, then gave him an apologetic look. 'But he only speaks Spanish.'

Ethan's shoulders slumped.

The dining room had a table with two chairs and a sofa near the television. Penny had failed to mention that the few channels the TV picked up were also only in Spanish, so after a while Ethan turned the TV off and curled up on the sofa. The excitement of getting his strength back was fast giving way to the effort of their adventure, and Ethan fell asleep.

Ethan woke up to Penny gently shaking his shoulder.

'How did it go?' he asked groggily.

'We're not sure yet,' replied Penny. 'He's rebooting, which will take some time. We couldn't quite repair him perfectly—'

'I just didn't have all the parts,' interrupted Professor Moore. 'There were at least two components in there that I'd never seen before.'

'We'll just have to wait and see,' said Penny.

'Are you hungry?' said Professor Moore. 'When he reactivates, I'll get a message on this.' She showed them the pager she was wearing on her hip. 'So we can relax for a while.'

Ethan's stomach was now fully awake, and growling.

Professor Moore's assistant, a small bald man with a thick moustache, brought in a tray of salteñas, which were small pockets of dough filled with chicken, vegetables and, as Ethan found out, a lot of spice. After two bites his mouth felt like it was on fire.

The professor handed Ethan a glass of milk. 'Sorry, I like them spicier than most. This will help.'

'It's getting late,' said Penny.

'Ethan, you can sleep here if that's okay with you,' said Professor Moore. 'Marco?'

The bald man reappeared.

'Could you bring Ethan some blankets, please?'

Marco left. 'There's a spare bed for you in my room, Penny,' said Professor Moore.

'I'm not sure I'll get much sleep, but thanks,' Penny replied.

'Do try. Goodnight, Ethan.'

Marco brought the blankets in as Penny and the professor left, and then nodded goodnight to Ethan.

Ethan snuggled in. He didn't think he'd be able to sleep, having just napped for a few hours, but he was instantly proven wrong.

CHAPTER 3

The dining area curtains were thin, and Ethan woke up with the sun. He stretched, yawned, and looked out the window to see Penny and Professor Moore running from the dormitory to the lab, pulling on dressing-gowns and slippers as they ran.

Ethan dragged on his shoes and dashed out to meet them.

'The reboot has finished,' said Penny.

They burst into the lab, and found Gemini sitting up and looking around him. Something about him was . . . different.

'Gemini?' said Penny, but he didn't react.

Penny got closer and took his hand. 'Gemini? It's me . . .'

Gemini looked at her. 'I'm very pleased to meet you, Gemini. I'm . . . actually, I'm not sure . . .'

'No,' said Penny slowly. '*You're* Gemini. My name is Penny.'

'Oh good. I'm still very pleased to meet you,' said Gemini.

Professor Moore looked at one of the read-outs. 'How do you feel, Gemini?'

'With my hands, mainly, but I have touch sensors all over my body.'

Ethan, Penny and Professor Moore looked at each other.

Penny said, 'Ethan, would you look inside him with your powers, please?'

Ethan closed his eyes. Gemini started to . . . giggle.

'HEEheeheehee, that tickles!'

Ethan had reached into Gemini before, but this looked very different. Gemini's internal network was a mess – where solid electronic pathways had glowed brightly before, now some were flickering, others dim. While he watched, he saw one flow of energy just stop completely and turn black with a sizzling sound.

'He's not in good shape,' said Ethan.

Professor Moore said, 'I'm so sorry, Penny. We did what we could, but I don't have the tools here that you do in your lab. According to these diagnostics, if you can't repair Gemini soon, his systems will break down beyond repair.'

Penny moved over to look at the same display. 'Nothing to apologise for, Jackie – I couldn't have done this much without you. So, we have about three days.'

'I need my lab,' Penny told Ethan. 'We have to get him back home.'

'To Titus?!' Ethan's jaw dropped. 'Right back into the National Service's hands?'

'I know it's dangerous, but it's the only place that has everything I need. And we have to get moving quickly.'

'A supply plane will be here in about an hour,' said Professor Moore.

Ethan looked worried. 'How will we get back? I can cover our electronic trail, but I'm pretty sure our photos will be at every airport in this part of the world.'

'Slim will be able to help,' the professor said. 'He's my main source for . . . well, everything, really. He uses some shady methods sometimes, but he gets what I need. He'll be piloting the supply plane.'

'Let's power Gemini down,' said Penny. 'That should slow the deterioration.'

Professor Moore flicked a switch and Gemini's wide eyes closed. She took Ethan and Penny back to the dining area for breakfast.

An hour later, the sound of a loud propellor engine whined towards the compound.

'Wait here,' said Professor Moore. 'I'll go talk to Slim.'

Ethan and Penny looked out the window to see the professor approach a thin man in a straw hat and a vest but no shirt.

They couldn't hear what she was saying, but the man walked back to his plane and then returned with a briefcase. Professor Moore led him into the dining area.

'My new friends,' he said, 'they call me Slim because if there's even a slim chance of getting something, I can get it. Professor Moore tells me you need some help with travel for the two of you and your amigo sleeping in the lab. So . . .'

He opened the briefcase to reveal twenty or so passports.

'Let's see what we can find, shall we?'

It took a few minutes, but they found three passports that came close enough to resembling the travellers-to-be.

Penny looked at the photo of one with the name *Margot Douglas*. 'Slim, do you have any blonde hair dye?'

Slim smiled. 'I have something even better: a wig as blonde as a blonde chihuahua!'

Ethan wondered if he could look close enough to thirteen years old to be Margot's son Ronnie. *If I slouch*, he thought, *and draw on some fake pimples* . . .

'Is there a hat or something I could have?' he asked, and Slim tossed him a baseball cap.

Gemini wasn't a bad match for Jack Douglas – the man in the photo on the ID page had a moustache, but they could just say he'd shaved it off. More concerning was the prospect of Gemini being able to pretend to be Jack.

As Penny fitted her wig and Ethan dotted his face with a borrowed lipstick, Professor Moore powered Gemini back up, instructing him to put on a denim shirt and a pair of cargo pants that were also provided by Slim.

As Gemini and Ethan boarded Slim's plane, the professor asked, 'So what do I owe you for the extras, Slim?'

Slim smiled. 'We'll settle up at the end of the month, as always, but it won't be cheap.'

Penny gave Professor Moore a warm hug and a heartfelt 'thank you', then boarded. She found Ethan sitting down, seatbelt on, and Gemini standing in the centre aisle, hunched due to the low ceiling.

Slim sat in the pilot seat and looked over his shoulder. 'Hey big guy, we're about to take off. Take a seat.'

Gemini's head tilted. 'May I have a spanner?'

'What?' Slim said.

'If I try to take one of these seats without undoing the bolts first, I will damage your plane.'

Penny whispered sharply, 'He means sit down.'

'Oh. Thank you, Gemini.'

'No,' said Penny wearily. 'You're Gemini, I'm Penny.'

Gemini sat next to Ethan, who did his seatbelt up for him.

The propellors turned faster and faster, and Slim took his passengers into the sky.

The flight to Bombara's main airport took about forty minutes. Gemini stayed completely still the whole time.

Slim brought the plane down with a bounce on a landing strip set apart from the international air traffic. He gave the fake Douglas family his best wishes, and they walked towards the terminal.

Once they were through the glass doors, Ethan scanned the departures board. He found the next flight to Titus, leaving in ninety minutes.

✈ Flight	Destination		Gate	Time
A01	SYDNEY		B2	10:05
Z32	BENIDORM		A1	10:35
F17	CENTROVA		--	11:25
R22	MOSCOW		--	11:52
C84	PRAGUE		:	13:24

'You know,' he said, 'we could go just about anywhere.'

Penny looked at Gemini. 'I need my tools to repair him. I need my lab.'

Ethan sighed. 'I was afraid you'd say that.'

He wished he could talk her out of having them return to Titus, but knew there was no way. He sent his powers through the terminal wi-fi and booked tickets for the Douglases.

They sat in a cafe and waited for the check-in counter to open.

'I guess you better do all the talking, Penny,' said Ethan. 'I don't know how to sound thirteen, and Gemini . . .'

'Good point. Gemini, we'll say that you can't talk because you've lost your voice.'

'Should I pretend to look for it?' said Gemini.

'Just stay quiet, please. We'll make it.'

They checked in for their flight. Penny did all the talking, while Ethan made sure that the airline computer didn't show any alerts. They received their boarding passes and handed over Penny and Ethan's backpacks. Ethan's backpack contained his helmet, headed for the cargo hold of the airliner.

At Customs, Penny took the lead again. The passport checking system was extra secure – Ethan, without his helmet, had to concentrate hard to make the travel records for all three passports look legitimate as they showed on the computer screen of the Customs officer.

The Customs officer frowned, and at one point tapped at her screen. Penny and Ethan held their breath.

With a flick of her hand, the officer waved them through.

As they joined the queue at the metal detector gates, Ethan and Penny breathed sighs of relief.

'You okay?' Penny asked Ethan, looking up at him. 'You look pale.'

'Bit of a headache. I guess I'm still getting used to having my power back on—'

BZZZ!

A sharp buzz cut Ethan's words off. Gemini, who had walked through the gate in front of them, had set off the metal detector.

'Of course – he's full of metal!' Ethan exclaimed.

Penny looked panicked as a security guard directed Gemini over for searching.

Ethan concentrated, and then all four metal detector gates started flashing and buzzing at random. The security guards didn't know who to start searching. The one closest to Gemini ushered him back to Ethan and Penny in the queue.

A guard flicked a switch, and all the gates went silent.

'Sorry, everyone,' said the security supervisor. 'We seem to have a problem with the metal detectors. Please be patient – we'll be turning them off and on again, and we'll get you moving as soon as possible.'

'I set the gate off,' said Gemini. 'Perhaps you should turn me off and on again instead.'

'Shhhh!' said Penny.

The gates were turned back on, and the queues started moving again. As Gemini walked through for the second time, Ethan reached into the system and made sure the gate stayed quiet.

They moved on to the departure lounge. Ethan's fake pimples were starting to itch, and he resisted the urge to scratch them. After a nervous wait, they boarded their flight, not knowing exactly what would be waiting for them back in Titus.

'Sir, we have another signal from Gemini.'

Agent Ferris walked over to look at the screen in front of Collins, the agent who had spoken.

'Where from this time?' he asked.

'His tracker must have been damaged. The signal is a little scrambled, but it looks as though he's at La Paz airport.'

Ferris frowned. *Either Penny's still running and Gemini is about to follow her to another country,* he thought, *or Gemini got her – and maybe E-Boy too – and is bringing them back.*

'Keep as close an eye as you can, Collins,' said Ferris. 'He's a valuable asset, chasing a valuable target – or targets. We need them back.'

CHAPTER 4

By halfway through the five-hour flight, Ethan was fed up with Gemini.

Gemini sat bolt upright in his seat, completely motionless, and after two hours of this other passengers had started to notice. Ethan told him to loosen up a little to look more natural, and Gemini had gone into a wriggle that looked like someone had filled his underwear with worms.

Then, when the flight attendant asked if Gemini wanted an apple turnover, he replied, 'No thank you, right way up is fine.'

Penny forced a laugh. 'That's just his sense of humour,' she said to the befuddled flight attendant. She then leaned in to Gemini's ear and told him to power down for the rest of the flight. 'Someone not moving doesn't draw as much attention if they look like they're sleeping.'

With other passengers so close, Ethan and Penny couldn't discuss any plans without the risk of being overheard, so they both did their best to relax until the plane started to descend into Titus's capital.

After the plane landed, they made their way carefully through the arrivals gate. Ethan kept the front of his cap pulled low as they walked past two National Service agents.

They went through Customs without a hitch, and with no metal detectors for incoming passengers they were soon walking towards the baggage collection carousels.

As they walked, Penny saw that Gemini was looking behind them and waving.

'Who are you waving to?' she asked.

'Those two men in the black suits. They've been watching us since we got off the plane.'

Ethan turned. The same two agents they had passed at the arrivals gate were following them.

'Guess our disguises weren't quite enough,' said Ethan.

One of the agents put his phone to his ear. Ethan reached across with his powers and cut both agents' phones from their mobile network.

The agent looked at his phone in annoyance, shook it, then put it in his pocket. He gestured to his colleague, and the other agent walked quickly to stand between the baggage carousels and the exit.

They were surrounded by tourists. As Ethan tried to make a plan, he overheard bits of conversation.

'Oh, I can't wait to get back into my own bed.'

'Straight back to work tomorrow – I really shoulda given myself another day or two off.'

'Son, hop off there, you don't know when that's going to start moving again.'

Ethan looked over and saw a father lifting his son off one of the baggage carousels.

Carousel number three was carrying the luggage from their flight, and as they'd been the last to check in for that flight their bags were the first to appear for collection.

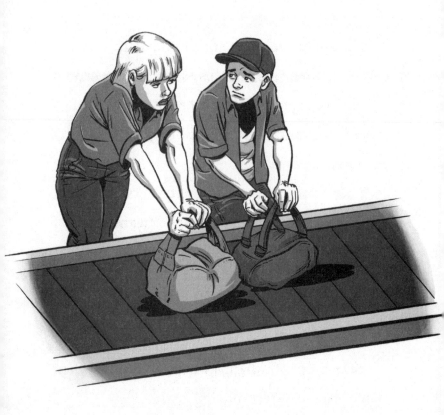

As soon as they grabbed their luggage, Ethan
held his hand near the carousel. It started to
move faster, as did the other four.

The other travellers looked around in surprise.
A couple of people extended hands for their bags
only to find them suddenly passing out of reach.

Whirring noises started to fill the hall as the motors that moved the carousels were pushed harder and faster than they'd been designed to.

Smaller bags started to roll off the carousels, then some of the larger cases as people began to back away behind seats and columns.

The agent near the exit looked to his partner for a signal of some sort. The partner made a move towards Penny, but a cello case launched off a carousel and swept his legs out from under him. Before he could get up, a heavy suitcase thumped onto him and knocked him out cold.

People started running in all directions. Some were trying to get away, others wanted to retrieve their luggage – a few were even grabbing whatever bags were nearby.

The agent near the door found himself swept outside by a stampede of fleeing travellers.

Ethan and Penny linked arms and grabbed Gemini, and rode the tide of people out the door, running for the rental car area while the agent was still tangled in other people.

The nearest car for rent was a blue family station wagon. The company had an online booking system, so using the company's own wi-fi Ethan forged a booking, and the three of them bundled into the car. Penny got behind the wheel and drove them away.

'Should I get us a hotel room?' asked Ethan.

'The longer we're here, the bigger the risk that we'll be caught before we can fix Gemini. We should go straight to the National Service base.'

Ethan gulped. 'Really? Surely after that mess they know we're here.'

Penny nodded. 'But they're not going to expect us to go straight to their home base. Plus, they still want me to work for them, so there's a chance that my security pass could get us in.'

Ethan took a deep breath, and decided he was sick of worrying. 'And if it doesn't, we'll figure something out. We always do.'

Penny smiled at Ethan. Gemini smiled at nothing in particular.

'Agent Ferris! Gemini's tracker has pinged again – they just left the airport!'

Agent Ferris rolled his eyes. 'Thank you very much, Agent Collins. Which airport?'

'Ours! They're here!'

Agent Ferris pressed a button on his phone. 'Alpha Team, meet me in the briefing room now.'

A few minutes later, Agent Ferris stood in front of six other agents. He handed them each a device with a screen, a number pad and a handgrip.

'All right, people, Gemini left ten days ago in pursuit of Penny Cook and E-Boy, and has now arrived back at the airport. It appears that his tracker transmitter has taken some damage, so we don't know what condition he's in. The devices you're holding will help track him. Pressing the thumb button will send a signal to his tracker, and it might reply and show you where he is. Be ready for anything – E-Boy and Doctor Cook may be with him.'

The agents all examined the devices.

'Now get your weapons,' said Agent Ferris, 'and wait for my order.'

As Alpha Team left the room, Collins came in.

'We just got a call from the airport. Two agents tried to intercept Gemini and Doctor Cook . . . they had a male with them. It appears that Gemini is travelling with them, maybe even working with them.'

Ferris thought about this for a second, then shook his head. 'No, he can't have switched sides. He wouldn't be sending tracking signals if he was working with Penny Cook. He must have her fooled.'

'The male,' said Collins. 'Could that be E-Boy?'

'Good chance. Get security footage from the airport, see what you can find. If we can get Gemini back, *and* catch Cook and E-Boy, President Bonner will be very happy.'

The main National Service centre was a plain-looking office building from the outside.

The front doors led to a public foyer, there was an emergency exit to the side that would only open from the inside, and there was an entrance to an underground carpark at the back. What people didn't notice was the array of security, the cameras and sensors that surrounded the building.

The station wagon was parked in a side street close to the main entrance, just barely in range of the wi-fi.

Ethan put on his helmet and reclined the back of his seat. 'I'm gonna need silence. Their system is really touchy, so I need to concentrate to not trigger anything.'

He let out a long slow breath, and closed his eyes.

He picked carefully through the National Service network, working hard to not leave any trace. After five minutes he said, 'No luck with

your security pass getting us in, Penny. There's an Arrest and Imprison On Sight order for you.'

Ethan didn't see Penny's disappointed frown. He did see the central processor for the security cameras, though, and had an idea.

'Penny,' he said, 'could you grab my laptop from my backpack and open it in front of me, please?'

Penny did so. Ethan raised his hands to the keyboard but didn't touch it. The computer turned on, and the screen was suddenly busy with windows opening and closing, and lines of code whizzing across.

'What are you doing?' asked Penny.

'Something that may help later. Let me concentrate.'

Ethan kept his focus until he felt the car lurch forwards, stop suddenly, then speed up again.

His eyes snapped open. Penny had pulled the car into traffic and was driving in a hurry.

'What's going on?' Ethan said.

'They found us!'

Ethan turned around to see three agents running up the street towards them, just as the agents were passed by three black cars.

The station wagon's tyres squealed as Penny turned onto the main road.

'I was sure I didn't trip any alarms!' said Ethan.

'Ethan, we need to get away! I didn't like the last car chase we were in, and I'm really not enjoying this one!'

'Well, I'll get rid of them like I did last time,' said Ethan, full of confidence.

He sent his concentration back and found the three National Service vehicles. He reached into the first one and switched off the electronic fuel injection, cutting off the petrol. It immediately lost speed and dropped back.

As soon as it slowed down, the other two cars vanished from the view of Ethan's powers.

Ethan turned around – the other black sedans were still approaching.

'C'mon, one down, two to go,' said Penny.

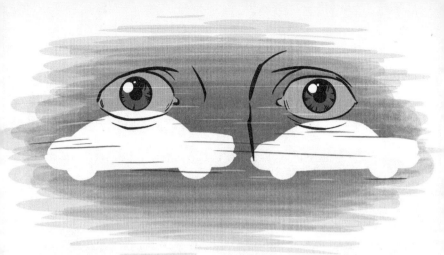

'I can't sense them,' said Ethan.

'They're right there!'

Ethan snapped, 'I can see them, but I can't find them with my powers!'

Since the chase during the Robofight Games, many National Service cars had been fitted with an isolator – a switch that shielded the vehicle from outside signals. No radio, no satnav . . . and no way in for E-Boy.

Penny gave a yelp as she hauled on the steering wheel, dragging the station wagon around a corner. The black cars kept up effortlessly.

'Okay, let's try this,' said Ethan. As Penny sped past a delivery van, Ethan found that it had electric power steering. He tugged on it just enough to waggle the front of the van towards the nearest agency car. The agent thought it was going to hit him, and veered into the kerb hard enough to burst two tyres.

The third black car dodged the accident and kept pursuing.

'Try not to use other people's cars, Ethan,' said Penny. 'It's too risky.'

Ethan looked around as the cars hurtled along the street. The traffic lights ahead turned red, so Penny gave another yelp and turned the station wagon down a small lane, then back out onto the main road.

The black car followed.

Ethan looked ahead, then concentrated. 'Penny,' he said, 'I need you to trust me. I need you to go through the next traffic lights, whatever colour they are.'

'What?!'

'Please. Trust me.'

In the last black car, the agent driving was unsure what to do. The isolator switch meant he couldn't radio for help, or tell anyone else where the car with Gemini in it was going.

He got the car closer to the station wagon as it approached the next traffic light. The light went from green to amber, but the station wagon didn't slow down.

This is crazy, the agent thought.

The light changed to red, and two seconds later the station wagon sped through the intersection.

The agent slammed on the brakes – he wasn't going to careen into the intersection when the traffic had started from the other direction. The black car stopped right on the white line.

Penny was pale, her mouth open.

She didn't dare check the rear-view mirror, but she was listening. No sound of a crash.

Ethan turned to look, then turned back and smiled.

'Ethan! That was so dangerous going through a red light like that!'

Ethan chuckled. 'It would've been . . . if I hadn't stopped the other light from turning green.'

Penny looked confused, then relaxed. 'The driver stopped because he thought cars were about to come, but you kept the other light red as well?'

'Until now.' Ethan let the other light turn green just as the agent pursuing them figured it out. Before he could restart the chase, the intersection between him and Penny's rental car was full of traffic.

Penny and Ethan breathed a sigh of relief.

'Do we know who else was in the car?' asked Ferris.

'No,' said Agent Collins as he looked at the security camera footage. 'They were parked too far away.'

Ferris tapped his chin. 'So we don't really know if Gemini is fooling Penny, or E-Boy, or both, or if he's actually switched sides . . . but why would he come here only to leave?'

The other agent didn't answer.

Ferris took out his phone and made a call. 'Where are we up to with the Aquarius project? We may need it soon.'

CHAPTER 5

Penny knew a coffee shop not far from where they had shaken off their pursuers. It had booths, so they could have some privacy as they spoke.

The breakfast rush had just finished, so the coffee shop was all but empty. A waitress greeted them with a friendly smile as they walked in.

'Hi, just sit yourselves anywhere, I'll get menus for you shortly.'

Penny spotted a booth in the far corner – the coffee shop would have to be near full before any customers would be in listening range.

'We need to figure out a way into the National Service building,' said Penny.

'I can take another look around Gemini's system, see if it's breaking down any faster,' said Ethan. 'Hopefully he won't giggle too loud – hang on, where is he?'

They realised Gemini wasn't walking with them to the booth. They spun around, and saw him sitting in a pot plant by the front door!

Ethan said, 'What on earth . . .'

Penny ran back to the front door and reached out to Gemini. 'When she said sit anywhere, she meant on a seat!'

Finally getting Gemini into the booth, Ethan sent his power in. The silver strands of Gemini's internal systems were darker and flickering more.

'Heeheeheehee!' giggled Gemini, much to Ethan's distraction. This time, Gemini's voice was high, making him sound like a laughing chipmunk.

'Gemini, say something,' said Penny.

'Something,' said Gemini, at about the pitch of a two-year-old child. 'My voice modulator seems to be damaged. Wait a moment.'

Gemini squinted, then spoke again. 'Is this any better?' This time he sounded like the lowest notes on a tuba.

Ethan looked at Penny with concern. 'You're the expert, but from what I saw I don't think it's long before he's completely . . .' He brought a finger across his lips and flicked it up and down, making a *blblblblblblblblblblblb* sound.

'I was unaware that I am even slightly *blblblblblblblblblblblb*,' said Gemini.

'Just don't talk,' said Ethan, pulling his laptop from his backpack. 'I don't know how to get us in yet, but I came up with something that'll help once we're there.'

He put a USB drive into the laptop and started a file transfer.

'When I was in the National Service system, I found the server that handles their security cameras. I got video of all of their corridors looking normal and copied it onto my computer.'

'So that's what you were doing when you asked me to get your laptop for you,' said Penny.

'Yep. This isn't something I've done before, but I think I can set up this USB stick so that if I can plug it into their system, it will show the video instead of the real view from the cameras.'

Penny was amazed. 'That's some complicated coding. How did you do it so quickly?'

Ethan shrugged. 'Dunno exactly. It's like . . . I've been stronger since not being linked to Gemini anymore. I don't code, I feel my way through what I want with my powers, and the code just kind of happens.'

'Well, let's hope it works,' said Penny.

'Gemini just pinged back again. Coffee shop on Trade Street.'

'Send whichever team is closest,' said Ferris.

Gemini watched as Penny and Ethan ate.

'We could always pretend we're delivering pizzas,' said Ethan. 'Get in that way.'

Penny gave a chuckle. 'While we're thinking, maybe you could go back into Gemini and try to even out that voice modulator.'

'Sure, I'll give it a go.'

Ethan waited for Gemini to start giggling again, and was surprised to see a large surge of energy in one of the circuits, which turned into a blinding silver flash that shot straight up and away.

'Gemini, did you just send a signal some-where?' asked Ethan.

'Yes.'

Ethan and Penny looked at each other. 'Why?'

'Once in a while,' said Gemini, 'a signal comes into my location tracker asking where I am, and I send one back giving my position.'

Ethan and Penny's jaws fell open.

'Who does it go to?' asked Penny.

'I don't know. Whoever sends the first signal.'

'*Where* does it go, then?' asked Ethan, getting annoyed.

'The most recent one went just outside,' said Gemini.

'*Just outside?!*' Ethan and Penny asked at the same time.

'Yes, seventy-one metres away.'

Ethan snuck over to the window and saw two agents closing in. One was carrying a taser, the other had a device Ethan didn't recognise.

Ethan turned to Penny and Gemini. 'National Service. We gotta go.'

Penny dropped some cash on the table to cover the bill, then led Gemini to the side door to the carpark. Penny opened the door and saw an agent take a taser from his jacket pocket.

Penny turned to Gemini. 'Do you think you can handle him?'

Gemini's head tilted. 'I don't see a problem.'

Gemini walked towards the agent as Penny motioned to Ethan to come over. As Ethan joined her, they watched as Gemini picked the hapless agent up and turned him every which way in his hands.

'What did you tell him to do?' said Ethan.

Penny pinched the bridge of her nose. 'Handle the agent.'

Ethan rolled his eyes as the agent struggled in Gemini's grip. The agent managed to press his taser into Gemini's side, but when he pushed the button Gemini just grinned widely and let out an *'Eeeeeeeeeeeeeeeee'* that reminded Ethan of a boiling kettle.

'Gemini,' said Ethan, 'give him a zap. With the taser. Please.'

Gemini did as Ethan said, and the agent crumpled to the ground, twitching.

The agent's black car was nearby. 'Put him in his car,' Ethan said to Gemini.

As Gemini bundled the agent into the back seat, Ethan put his hand against the dashboard and felt the car's electronics, including the isolator switch. *That explains why I couldn't stop the cars during the chase*, he thought.

Penny looked back into the coffee shop and watched as the other two agents spoke to the waitress.

Ethan kicked at the isolator switch until it broke, locked the car doors, then used his power to activate the isolator. It was a weird feeling – the car was obviously still in front of him, but to his powers it felt like it had vanished.

'Let's go,' he said.

Agent Ferris was furious.

'I know your remote won't open the car, the isolator blocks all signals in and out. All of them. No, you won't be able to break a window and get him out, they're reinforced. Now, do you want to tell me why you didn't leave him in the car, and find Gemini and whoever he's with?'

Ferris hung up before the agent could answer.

'Gemini,' asked Penny, 'how often do you receive one of those travelling signals?'

They had driven to a petrol station. Ethan was in the restroom washing the fake pimples off his face while Penny and Gemini stayed in the car.

'It varies,' said Gemini, his high-pitched tone back. It made him sound like a chirping bird.

'Because my receiver is damaged, I can't be certain how many times they send a signal before I detect it.'

Ethan returned and got into the front passenger seat, rubbing his freshly cleaned face.

'And when that locator signal comes in,' Penny said, 'do you have to answer or can you choose?'

'I could choose,' said Gemini. 'It didn't occur to me not to respond. Should I ignore the signal next time?'

'Yes!' said Ethan.

'No,' said Penny.

Ethan looked at her surprised. 'Seriously?'

'I have an idea of how to get into the National Service base.'

CHAPTER 6

'Ping it again,' said Ferris.

'Sir, I can, but it's been less than a minute since I tried—'

'I know. I was here when you did it. Ping it again.'

The agent pressed the button on the tracker. 'It's working.'

'So where's Gemini?'

The agent frowned. 'He's at . . . the front door!'

Ferris ran to the front door and saw agents surrounding Gemini and Penny.

'Gemini,' said Ferris, 'what's going on?'

Gemini looked at Ferris. 'I've been pursuing Doctor Cook and hah . . . her associate E-Boy.

I hahahaven't been able to capture E-Boy, but I was able to bring Doctor Cook back.'

Ferris raised an eyebrow. 'Did something happen to your voice?'

'I was damaged in a fall from a plaaaaane, but I am functional enough for now.'

Ferris stepped closer.

'What do you mean, "for now"?'

'My systems are breaking down, and I am in neeheeheeheed of urgent repairs,' said Gemini.

'We can have Doctor Ross here within the hour. Are you actually laughing?'

'I could have a look if you'd like,' said Penny.

'Great,' said Ferris. 'This is a laughing robot, and she's trying to tell jokes. We'll be taking you to your room, Doctor Cook, and you'll be staying there. If Doctor Ross needs your help, he will shout questions to you through your very locked door.'

Ferris looked at one of the other agents. 'Right. It goes to the lab, she goes to her cell.'

Two agents took Penny by the arms while two more kept her boxed in as they led her inside. The remaining agent accompanied Gemini.

As they all went indoors, Ethan poked his head out from behind a parked van.

He'd been able to control Gemini from a short distance, but his powers couldn't keep him connected past the door.

Just hold it together, metal man, thought Ethan. *You have one job. Do it and everything will be . . . well, we'll have a chance, anyway.*

Ethan walked around the building, towards the rear entrance.

Penny didn't say another word on the way back to her room.

She looked at the bars on the windows and gave a heavy sigh. Until her door opened there was nothing she could do, and Gemini was getting worse every minute.

Ethan and Gemini working together . . . they could be amazing!

We need to get through this first, though.

'Doctor Ross will be here in about forty minutes,' said the agent who had accompanied him.

Gemini nodded. He remembered Ethan's first instruction: *don't say anything without me.*

The agent left, and Gemini looked at all the machines around him. He recognised some of the devices; others were a complete mystery.

He looked for that one slot.

There.

Gemini took Ethan's USB stick from his pocket and wiggled it into the port in the audio sense tester. *Anywhere it'll fit will do,* Ethan had said.

Gemini watched as a tiny light on the end of the drive started to flash.

Ethan sat near the opening to the underground carpark, focused on the building's network, just occasionally looking around the laneway.

He found the security circuits. He wasn't sure what it would look like, but he thought – hoped, maybe – that he would spot when Gemini put his drive into the system.

If he can, Ethan thought. *And if it works.*

He hoped Penny was okay. At least he was outside while he waited, and not stuck in a cell like she was – a cell she had been stuck in before. *Gotta be driving her mad.*

Ethan watched as energy shot along the security network in random pulses. A rumble of a car engine grabbed his attention, and he moved away from the carpark entrance just as a black sedan rolled out and away.

Ethan tapped back into the building's wi-fi and noticed that the energy pulses were now coming in a set pattern, not random anymore.

That must be it, he thought. *Their screens should be showing what I copied.*

He stood up and crept into the carpark – avoiding the cameras wouldn't help if a live person spotted him.

A black sedan appeared on the ramp behind him and he jumped behind a parked car. The sedan found a space to stop in and a sole agent got out.

As the agent walked for the door, Ethan crept behind him. The agent used a touch card to open a heavy-looking door and entered the building. Ethan snuck up and through the door before it shut.

Penny paced the floor. It felt like the walls were closing in.

It was getting harder to keep her composure. There were so many things that could go wrong, and she wouldn't know . . . all that would happen was that she'd be stuck here, and she might never find out which stage of the plan had gone wrong, if Gemini had fallen too far apart, if Ethan had gotten—

The door to the cell slid open without warning, making Penny jump. On the other side was . . .

'It worked!' said Penny.

'Well, I'm here. Let me deal with the camera in here, then we'd better move.'

Ethan's power interfered with the camera – not enough to shut it down completely, but enough to make it hard to see with. He and Penny then snuck out and along the corridor.

Doctor Jakoby Ross was nervous.

The phone call he'd received made it sound like Gemini was seriously damaged. He knew how valuable Gemini was to President Bonner and the government – if he couldn't fix Gemini, who knew what would happen to him, Ross?

Doctor Ross stood at the door to the lab, took a deep breath, swallowed, and opened the door.

Sitting on the lab workbench, back in his suit, was Gemini. He had wider eyes and a far wider smile than Ross was expecting.

Doctor Ross stepped inside. 'Hello Gemini, what's happening?'

'Well,' said Gemini, 'I'm about to tie you to a chair and gag you.'

'Wait, what?'

Doctor Ross heard the door shut, and spun around. Standing in front of the now-locked door were Ethan and Penny.

'Ross just arrived,' said Agent Ferris. 'I'll let him work for about an hour, then ask for a status report.'

'Can he do it?' asked President Bonner.

'We'll have to see. It would be better if we could trust Doctor Cook, but we'll work with what we have.'

'If Aquarius lives up to expectations, we may not need Gemini. How long before Aquarius is operational?' asked President Bonner.

'The tech team wants to run some more tests,' said Ferris, 'but it should be any day now.'

'All right, do whatever you need to get Aquarius online as quickly as possible. I'm giving you full authorisation – money, personnel, whatever is necessary to make Project Aquarius fully operational.'

'I understand, sir,' Ferris said. 'I'll keep you updated.'

'I hope you're comfortable, Jakoby,' said Penny. 'This will take a while.'

Doctor Ross didn't look comfortable. Or happy.

Penny attached the last of the sensors to Gemini's head, then powered him down. Ethan watched as she took a section of Gemini's chest and lifted it off, revealing circuit boards that smelled faintly of smoke. She took a circuit board out and carried it over to a microscope, giving a disappointed sigh as she looked through it.

Over the next ninety minutes, Ethan got to watch Penny working up close. He was impressed. Doctor Ross was impressed too, although he would never admit it.

Penny gently fitted Gemini back together, then plugged three devices into different ports on Gemini's body, plus one more into his head.

'We don't have to wait overnight again, do we?' asked Ethan.

'No,' said Penny. 'I have better instruments here than at Jackie's. We'll know a lot sooner than that. I think it went well, but we'll have to see.'

There was a faint buzzing noise that made Ethan look around. Penny listened close to Gemini to make sure it wasn't coming from him.

Ethan tracked it down.

Doctor Ross's phone was ringing in his pocket. Ethan took it out and checked the screen.

'Four missed calls,' said Ethan. 'That's not good.'

Ferris ended his fourth attempt to call Doctor Ross.

'Should we go to the lab?' asked Agent Collins.

Ferris shook his head. 'He's doing delicate work. We don't want to disturb him if we don't have to.'

'Should we keep an eye on Doctor Cook?' asked Collins.

Ferris tapped at his computer – the video from the camera in Penny's cell was distorted.

'Tell the duty patrol to swing by Cook's room,' said Ferris. 'Knock, but don't barge in. We still hope we can turn her around to work for us again.'

Agent Collins sent a text message to the agent patrolling the nearest corridors. A minute and a half later, a text came back.

No answer to knock. Enter?

Ferris brought up the vision from a security camera that pointed straight at Penny's door, but couldn't see anyone. 'Is he sure he's at the right door?'

Collins passed on the message. The reply came back quickly. *214D, sir?*

Ferris looked at Penny's door, with *214D* painted on it. Still no sign of the patrolling agent, though.

Ferris's phone rang – it was Agent Hunt, the man who had been tasered by Gemini and locked in his own car by Ethan.

'Sir,' said Hunt, 'I just got free from my car – they're working together! Gemini, Doctor Cook and a third person, who I can only assume is E-Boy . . . they're a team!'

Ferris looked at the screen. *They must be messing with the security cameras! That's why I can't see the agent at Cook's door.*

Ferris hit a big red button on the desk.

'Intruders on base, code red,' he said into the microphone. 'Capture Gemini, Penny Cook, and anyone with them on sight. I repeat: code red, capture Gemini, Penny Cook and anyone with them on sight!'

He turned to Collins. 'Activate Aquarius.'

'Are you sure Aquarius is ready?'

'Let's call this a field test. I think Cook got herself captured because she needed her lab to repair Gemini. If she's succeeded, then Gemini is back under her control, not ours, and that makes it dangerous. Not just for what it can do, but what it might know.

'So, Collins,' Ferris continued, 'unless you need more of an explanation to follow an order, activate Aquarius.'

'Turning his background systems back on,' said Penny. 'Ethan, would you mind having a look?'

Ethan sent his powers into Gemini, and this time Gemini didn't giggle. Ethan still saw damage to Gemini's systems, but instead of circuits fading then turning black, this time the light was growing stronger. Some dark sections of Gemini's electronic pathways were starting to flicker back to life.

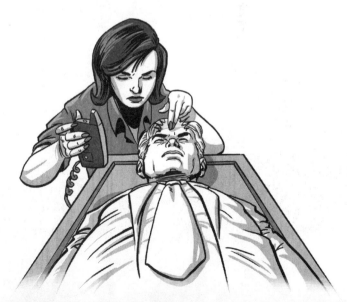

'Near as I can tell,' said Ethan, 'he's patching himself back together.'

'Patching *himself* back together?' said Penny with a smile. 'Don't I get any credit—'

A loud alarm cut off all conversation.

'Intruders on base, code red,' said a voice over the PA system. 'Capture Gemini, Penny Cook, and anyone with them on sight. I repeat: code red, capture Gemini, Penny Cook and anyone with them on sight!'

'I guess we've been found out,' said Ethan.

'I can't activate Gemini fully,' said Penny. 'It's too soon, he'd take all that damage again and then some.'

Ethan looked at Doctor Ross, who seemed to be smiling.

'I'll get him able to walk,' she continued, 'but I'll need your help controlling him.'

'What are you so happy about?' Ethan asked Doctor Ross as he removed his gag.

'Apart from the fact that this means I'll be untied soon, I might get to see my most impressive project in action.'

'What project?' asked Penny.

'Oh, you'll know it if you see it. You know, if you surrender to me and I take you to Agent Ferris, he'll probably show some leniency.'

Ethan put Doctor Ross's gag back in. 'Can you get Gemini's night vision working?' he asked Penny as he put on his helmet.

'Yes – but if I get function going in his eyes and legs, I won't be able to start up anything else without him short-circuiting.'

'Fingers crossed that'll be all we need,' said Ethan.

He opened the door to the corridor, and guided Gemini forwards. Ethan used his abilities to look through Gemini's eyes as the three of them snuck out of the lab.

They heard footsteps running towards them. Ethan concentrated, and turned out every light in the building. The corridor echoed with the sound of slipping feet and bodies hitting walls. Using Gemini's night vision, Ethan saw a tangle of five agents who had fallen over each other in the darkness.

'Can you guide us outta here?' asked Ethan.

'I think so,' said Penny.

They crept on slowly. A single agent inched towards them carrying his taser, not knowing they were there. Ethan focused on the taser, then said, '*Boo!*'

The agent and Penny both jumped. The agent hit the button on his taser, and Ethan redirected the electrical charge into the taser's handle.

The agent shuddered and twitched his way to the floor.

Ferris tapped a button on his computer, switching the vision from one security camera to the next, none of them showing the real picture of what was happening. He grunted in frustration. He tapped a different button and brought up a map of the building.

'Lab is there . . .' he mumbled to himself. 'Exit is there . . . Collins!'

Collins snapped to attention.

'The most direct path out from Cook's lab is via this emergency exit. Place Aquarius there, now.'

The blackout Ethan created covered them nicely.

Every few minutes a group of agents would approach, but as long as Ethan, Gemini and Penny stayed still and silent, they would pass without any more alarm.

'Are we nearly out?' whispered Ethan.

'Pretty sure,' said Penny. 'Just another couple of turns.'

They rounded a corner, and Ethan saw a figure standing close to the emergency exit. He stopped Gemini from going any further.

'I think there's a problem with Gemini's eyes, or his optical circuits, or something. There's something here that's not right.'

'What are you seeing?' asked Penny.

Ethan didn't answer. He listened, but couldn't hear any footsteps nearby. It looked like no one else was in the immediate area, just this lone figure ahead.

Ethan turned the lights back on, so he could see with his own eyes instead of Gemini's.

The figure stopped Ethan and Penny in their tracks. It looked just like Gemini.

But bigger.

'*What is that?!*' shouted Ethan.

'I am Aquarius,' the figure said. 'You will lie down on the floor. Now.'

Aquarius raised his left hand. His fingertips slid back, but instead of surgical instruments, out popped the tips of four darts.

Aquarius aimed his hand at the group. The darts fired.

One went straight up and stuck in the ceiling above Aquarius's head.

Two crossed over and hit the walls.

The fourth flew almost straight, and embedded in the shoulder of an agent who was sneaking up on Penny.

The agent crumpled to the ground, and started snoring.

Agent Ferris's
computer showed a feed
straight from Aquarius's eyes.

Next time, we test the weapons first, thought
Ferris.

Ethan couldn't help it – he chuckled a little.

Aquarius lowered his left hand and raised his
right. This time it wasn't darts that appeared when
the fingertips moved, but four long thin blades.

Ethan stopped smiling, and concentrated.

He only got a glimpse into Aquarius's systems before they went dark, just like the cars that chased them earlier.

I'm getting sick of these isolator things, Ethan thought.

Agent Ferris's screen went black.

Aquarius's isolator switch has been triggered, he thought. *Whoever that is hiding behind Gemini must be E-Boy!*

Ferris tapped at his keyboard, switching the video from Aquarius's inactive connection to one of the security cameras in the area, but it was showing the same bogus footage as before.

Ferris slammed his fist onto his desk, then brought Aquarius's inactive video feed back onto the screen, waiting for him to reconnect.

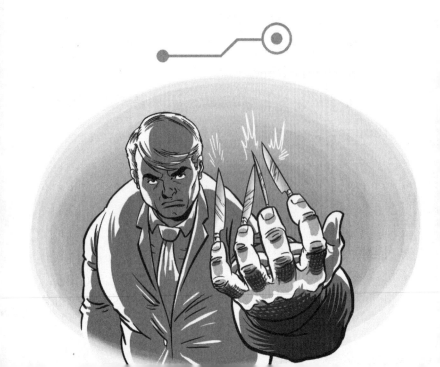

Aquarius walked towards the team.

Ethan looked up, then looked at the agent still snoring at his feet.

With a flex of his powers, Ethan put out the lights again, then activated the fire sprinkler above Aquarius's head. As Aquarius looked up, Ethan crouched and grabbed the taser from the agent on the floor. He fired it at Aquarius's head.

Electricity crackled all around Aquarius as the electricity of the taser hit the water from the sprinkler. Aquarius's arms flailed around him as light arced in every direction.

Ethan pushed Gemini into a side corridor, and Penny followed. As the electrical bolts faded, Aquarius gave chase. As he ran down the corridor, he sped past a doorway that Ethan, Penny and Gemini were hiding in. The team inched their way back towards the emergency exit.

As Ethan pushed the bar to open the exit door, light poured in from the other side – the lights in the emergency exit staircase must be on a different circuit from the rest of the corridors. The light and the noise of the door attracted Aquarius's attention, and the massive robot turned to run straight after them.

They were one floor above street level and bolting down the stairs. As Ethan guided Gemini's feet off the steps and onto the ground floor, Aquarius burst into the stairwell and jumped, landing with a booming thud at the bottom of the stairs. Penny shoved the door to the street open . . . and Aquarius stopped.

Agent Ferris's screen showed the team enter the emergency exit stairwell, as Aquarius turned his system isolator off.

Ferris watched as Aquarius leaped and landed, and spotted Penny opening the door to the outside.

'*Aquarius, stop!*' Ferris shouted into his desk microphone.

'Um . . . sir?' said Collins.

'We can't let Aquarius be seen outside,' said Ferris. 'There are bigger plans.'

He shook his head in fury as Ethan bustled Gemini and Penny through the door and onto the street.

CHAPTER 7

They had taken the station wagon to a cheap motel surrounded by factories, and booked into a room with two beds. Gemini lay on one, unmoving. Ethan lay on the other, holding his head.

Penny stomped her way around the room, furious.

'Ross dared to call that thing *his* project?! He's obviously used my notes, my data, my research . . . The nerve of him!'

Ethan winced. 'I know you're angry, but could you keep it down? I got a massive headache using my powers all those different ways.'

Penny sighed. 'Sorry, Ethan. It's just so infuriating. Why do you think Aquarius stopped chasing us?'

'Dunno, but I don't think he's stopped for good. How's Gemini looking?'

'I was hoping you could tell me,' said Penny.

'In a few minutes, if that's okay. Just need to wait for my head to stop throbbing.'

'Actually,' said Gemini with his eyes still closed, 'I can update you myself.'

Penny and Ethan turned to Gemini.

'I didn't think you'd be able to talk yet,' said Penny.

Gemini said, 'I can decide where to send my energy – if I do not need to move or solve complex problems, I am able to talk.'

Penny smiled. 'How are your systems?'

'Still coming back online, but all satisfactory so far. I cannot yet judge how close I will return to my full capacity, but you can be assured I won't be sitting in any more pot plants anytime soon.'

Ethan chuckled. 'You remember that, huh?'

'Yes,' said Gemini. 'I have complete memories of everything since rebooting in Professor Moore's laboratory in Bombara.'

He turned his head to Penny. 'Doctor Cook, when I think of that incident, I experience a sensation I have never known. I believe you would call it . . . embarrassment?'

'That's okay, Gemini,' said Penny. 'People do silly things all the time. What are your thoughts on Aquarius?'

'Dangerous,' said Gemini. 'From what we saw, Aquarius is faster than I am, and has weapons that will be very effective once they're finetuned. As Doctor Ross has obviously used my specifications as a starting point, I would suggest that Aquarius is superior to me in almost every way.'

Ethan's shoulders slumped. 'Well, that's a cheery thought.'

'Doctor Cook, with your permission, I will now power down and let my systems focus on repairing and restarting my system, rather than splitting my energy like this any longer.'

'Of course,' said Penny.

Gemini closed his eyes.

Ethan said, 'Looks like he's getting back to normal. I don't feel any weaker . . . I guess that means that link between us got broken.'

'That's good,' said Penny.

'If he starts up again and he's fine, can we go? I mean, I'm nervous being this close to National Service headquarters, this far away from my parents, and I don't really think we're ready to take on President Bonner yet.'

Penny nodded. 'Maybe we could set up with Jackie Moore in Bombara if she'll have us. Take time to make the lab we need, rather than be in a hurry like last time.'

'Yeah,' said Ethan. 'Be nice to not be running for a while. And we can't stay here.'

'I'm not happy about this,' said Doctor Ross.

Ferris rolled his eyes. 'You gave Aquarius Gemini's face as a message to Cook. Fine. She got that message. But thanks to the Robofight Games, Gemini's face is famous. Everyone knows it's government-issue, and we don't want people knowing Aquarius is ours as well. Not yet, anyway.'

'How are its weapons?'

'Better,' said Ross. 'Still some minor adjustments to be made, but they're better.'

Ferris's phone rang. Collins's voice said, 'We've found them.'

Ferris met Collins in the City-Wide Observation Room. The walls were lined with screens – the four biggest ones showed Ethan, Penny and Gemini leaving the National Service Centre, getting into the station wagon, the wagon driving away, and the wagon parked in the motel carpark.

Ferris smiled, and pointed to the fourth screen. 'Zoom out on this one.'

Collins tapped at a keyboard and the motel grew smaller, taking in more of the surrounding area.

'Okay,' said Ferris, as he tapped the screen on what looked like a warehouse roof, close to the motel. 'Do you know what that building is?'

'No,' said Collins. 'Should I?'

'Probably not. Send a five-agent team, plus Aquarius. If Aquarius can destroy Gemini, that'll show that we don't need Gemini or Cook anymore.'

CHAPTER 8

Penny couldn't sleep. Ethan could: his efforts during the day had left him exhausted. Penny just watched Gemini, waiting for him to finish rebooting.

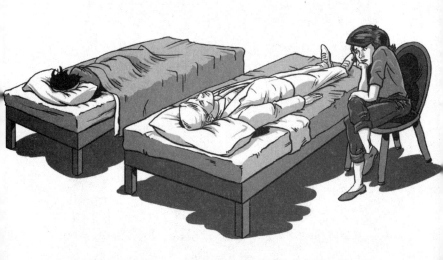

Without her lab, she couldn't give Gemini a thorough system check, but if Ethan could tell her that Gemini wasn't breaking down anymore then that wouldn't matter so much.

Outside the window, a chain link fence separated their motel from the overgrown grass of a huge vacant lot. There was no wind, but Penny heard the fence rattle, and then a thud of something hitting the ground.

'Ethan,' said Penny, shaking him awake. 'Someone's outside.'

Ethan shook his head to clear it. 'You sure?'

'I'm pretty sure I just heard someone climb the fence.'

Ethan looked out the window. 'I can't sense a phone, or anything electronic.'

But what he saw was two hands grip the bottom of the window and force it upwards, breaking the lock in the process.

A massive figure climbed in and stood in front of Ethan and Penny.

'Another giant?!' said Ethan.

'No,' said Gemini as he rose from the bed. 'This is the same giant, but with a different face. This is Aquarius.'

Ethan took Penny by the shoulders and ushered her to a corner of the room. He searched the area with his powers as Gemini and Aquarius faced off.

'Five agents nearby,' he said. 'I can feel their tasers and phones.'

'Gemini,' said Penny urgently, 'how are you?'

'Systems at ninety-eight per cent,' said Gemini. 'I will deal with Aquarius as well as I can, but am unable to protect you at the same time.'

'Don't worry about us,' said Ethan. 'Just concentrate on turning that metal goon into scrap.'

Gemini raised his right hand and activated the laser scalpels in his fingertips. Aquarius brought out his fingertip blades, and a clicking sound in his left hand revealed a mirror in his palm.

The next few seconds were a blur.

Gemini attacked, hands and feet flying, using the martial arts programmed into him for the Robofight Games. Aquarius countered with exactly the same programming.

Gemini punched, Aquarius blocked. Aquarius kicked, Gemini ducked.

Gemini jabbed with the lasers, and the mirror in Aquarius's palm reflected them upwards where they burned into the ceiling.

'You should leave,' said Gemini as he crashed his shoulder into Aquarius's midriff, then grabbed Aquarius's arm and tried to flip him.

Aquarius turned the fall into an easy cartwheel and stood ready for more combat.

'The agents are coming to the front door,' said Ethan. 'We better go out the window.'

Ethan helped Penny to the outside as Aquarius grabbed Gemini's attempt at a punch and threw him through the door.

Ethan boosted Penny up the chain link fence. She sat on top, looking back at the motel room. 'Something's not right.'

'Something other than two human-looking robots destroying each other in a motel?' said Ethan.

They heard footsteps closing in, and bolted for the vacant lot.

Objective 1 – protect Penny and Ethan

Objective 2 – disable Aquarius

Objective 3 – protect own hardware

Gemini moved his head out of the way of a devastating punch just in time.

Gemini kicked Aquarius's leg out from under him, and on his way down Aquarius slashed into Gemini's leg with his blades.

Damage – minor

Gemini rolled up and back to his feet, then ran out of the motel.

Ethan and Penny crunched their way through the dry grass of the vacant lot as the agents came after them, torches flashing. In the darkness, Penny lost a shoe – this slowed them down, but the chase continued.

After two more minutes, Penny asked, 'Have they gotten any closer?'

'I don't think so,' panted Ethan.

'And they're not trying to surround us, are they?'

'No, they're all in one clump.'

Penny stopped. 'They're not trying to capture us, they're just herding us away . . . away from Gemini!'

'Why?' said Ethan.

'I guess they want to keep Gemini and Aquarius's fight one-on-one. It's a test.'

They had reached the fence at the far end of the vacant lot. On the other side was a used car showroom.

'Well,' said Ethan, 'let's get back to him then.'

Ethan's powers found a single electric car among the vehicles for sale. He only sensed two other cars – either it was a nearly-empty

showroom, or the other cars were too old to have many electronic parts. Ethan turned the electric car on, and started moving it towards them.

The agents were close enough to be seen past their torches. They kept their tasers holstered, but were reaching for batons and handcuffs.

Ethan felt the car straining against an obstacle, not driving freely, and focused harder.

The agents got closer, handcuffs opened and ready to snap on wrists.

From behind the fence there came an enormous **CRASH**.

The electric car burst through the glass wall of the showroom, and the agents froze in the headlights.

Ethan grabbed Penny and pulled her aside as the car crunched through the fence, sending the agents leaping and scattering.

The car's doors opened and Penny and Ethan jumped in, clambering to get into the seats as the car sped through the grass. The wheels kicked up a tonne of dust as the car turned and sped off, thumping over the kerb as it hit the road.

'Where are they?' said Penny.

Ethan felt for Gemini, then commanded the car's GPS to show him. He grunted with the effort – his helmet was back in the motel room.

'There,' said Ethan. 'I guess it's a factory or something – it's massive, whatever it is.'

'Let's hope we get there in time,' said Penny.

Gemini's lasers whizzed at Aquarius's face. Aquarius ducked and took a step back. Gemini closed in and threw a fake punch, bringing his knee up instead and catching Aquarius on the hip, driving him further towards a four-storey building looming behind him.

Penny and Ethan are not in range. May need to disengage from fight to make sure they are not in danger.

Gemini stopped moving forwards, ready to defend himself from an attack while he calculated where his partners might be.

Aquarius also stopped. After a moment he took two more steps backwards towards the building, then stopped again.

Gemini analysed Aquarius's movements. *Aquarius appears to be trying to lure me into that building. Disengage.*

Gemini turned to run back towards the motel. Aquarius took two steps and then jumped clear over Gemini's head, twisting as he did.

Aquarius landed, immediately firing off a series of punches and swipes with his finger blades.

Damage – chest, minor

Right arm – medium

Left ear – medium

Aquarius appears to be fighting harder and faster. Conclusion – he was not fighting to his fullest previously.

Aquarius jumped again, kicking Gemini three times in mid-air and sending him clear through the outer wall of the building.

Ethan and Penny drove up to the huge building, and saw the hole in the wall.

'That can't be good,' said Ethan.

They got out of the car and climbed in through the hole, finding themselves in a long corridor. To the right were clean walls and unscuffed floors. To the left . . .

The damage was all around: walls, ceiling and floor. Wires and plaster hung from the walls; the lights overhead were either broken or flickering. Ethan looked down. 'Is that oil?'

Penny's hand went to her mouth.

They followed the oil trail around a corner, arriving at a bent steel door that was hanging from its hinges. Ethan moved it aside and they stepped through to what looked like a control room, with every computer, screen and keyboard trashed.

On the far side was a huge gap where a window used to be.

'What the . . . ?' said Ethan.

Penny ran up to the window gap, and looked down a ten-metre drop to a room the size of five basketball courts. On the concrete floor below, still fighting, were Aquarius and Gemini.

Gemini was clearly taking the worst of it.

Gemini threw two punches and an elbow; Aquarius blocked both punches and grabbed the elbow, throwing Gemini to the ground with it.

'There's nothing electronic nearby,' said Ethan. 'I can't help him!'

'GEMINI!' shouted Penny.

Arm damage – severe

Vision – down to half

Mobility – down to a third

'GEMINI!'

Gemini looked up, and saw Penny at the broken window.

'Gemini, he has the same combat programs as you. So don't use them! Do what makes you different – think of something *else!*'

Gemini looked at Aquarius, who was preparing to finish the job.

Gemini went to throw a punch with his right arm, but it hung limp at the elbow, flapping uselessly into Aquarius's chest.

Aquarius moved to Gemini's right, near the vulnerable arm. Gemini brought his left hand up to his own mouth and flicked his forefinger between his lips. '*Blblblblblblblb.*'

Aquarius twitched, scanning his combat programs for a move that this could possibly be leading to.

In a flash, Gemini's right hand flew up and pulled Aquarius's mouth open. He plunged his left hand into Aquarius's open mouth and activated his laser scalpels, damaging Aquarius's internals.

In the control room, Ethan saw the energy suddenly flowing through Aquarius's systems. 'He trashed the isolator circuit!' He reached in with his power and brought Aquarius to a complete stop.

Gemini jumped and sliced Aquarius in half, sending sparks and oil everywhere.

Both robots collapsed to the floor. Only Gemini got back up.

CHAPTER 9

Penny dashed out of the control room, looking for a way down to Gemini. Ethan scanned the area with his powers, and found that the ceiling and walls were dotted with video cameras. *That fight was always meant to happen here,* thought Ethan. *So someone could watch.*

As Penny ran to Gemini's side, Ethan short-circuited all the cameras.

Ferris watched on his office computer as Gemini got back to his feet. The screen went black.

'That was disappointing,' said Ferris, 'but educational.'

'I'm sorry,' said Doctor Ross.

'Don't be sorry – yet. We have too much invested to stop Project Aquarius now. If there's another failure, though, that'll be the time to be sorry.'

Ethan found the way down to the larger room, where Penny was checking Gemini's damage.

'I will need extensive repairs,' said Gemini, 'but my processors are undamaged.'

'That's gotta be a relief,' said Ethan. 'Can you walk?'

'Yes, but only at roughly one-third of my usual pace.'

'Well, we'd probably better get going then,' said Penny.

'First, I just wish to say . . .' Gemini paused. 'Thanks to your repairs, I now have complete memories of all that has happened since the lightning strike that gave Ethan his powers. I am aware of all that I have done, and all that I have tried to do.'

Penny put her hand on Gemini's shoulder.

Gemini continued. 'This seems to be a more intense version of that embarrassment I sensed earlier. I . . . am sorry.'

'You had so many people interfering with your programming,' said Penny. 'You don't need to apologise.'

Gemini looked into her eyes, and just for a moment there was something unrobotic about the gaze. Something a little too human. Penny quickly looked away.

Ethan felt awkward standing nearby while Penny and Gemini had their moment. He scanned the room, and something grabbed his attention. 'What's through there?' he asked.

Penny and Gemini turned. Ethan was looking at a large set of double doors. The glow underneath showed that there was a light switched on on the other side of them.

'Let's not get too curious,' said Penny. 'We have no idea what could be in there.'

'I'm not picking up any signals from the other side.' Ethan walked up and pressed his ear to one of the doors. 'No noises, either.'

'I also am detecting no sound from the next room,' said Gemini. 'There would appear to be no immediate threat.'

'But . . .' said Penny, but Ethan was already turning the handle.

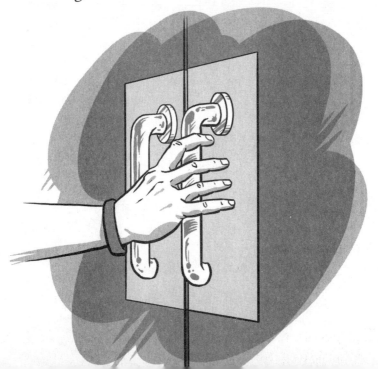

The sight left everyone speechless.

Gemini saw his own face, over and over and over again.

Standing in rows, unmoving, blankly staring forwards, were at least a hundred Aquarius robots.

For what seemed like forever, no one moved.

Eventually, Penny said, 'This . . .'

Ethan finished for her. 'This is bad.'

'Very bad,' said Gemini.

TO BE CONTINUED . . .

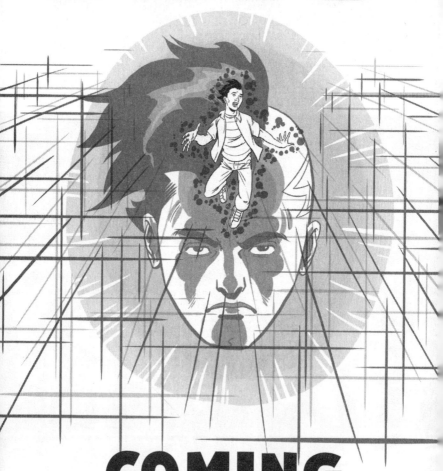

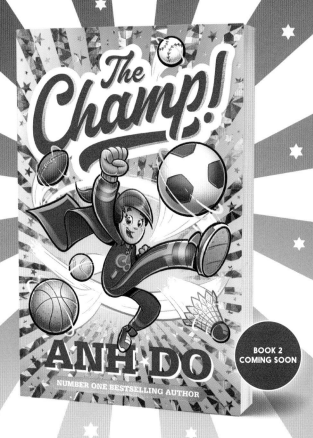